THIS BOOK BELONGS TO:

_____

TO READ WITH:

_____

To Lottie Boss

PICTURE SQUIRRELS

Published in 2016 in Great Britain by Barrington Stoke Ltd
18 Walker Street, Edinburgh, EH3 7LP

www.picturesquirrels.co.uk

Text © 1992 Alexander McCall Smith
Illustrations © 2016 Zoe Persico

A CIP catalogue record for this book is available
from the British Library upon request

ISBN 978-1-78112-514-4

Printed in China by Leo

BOING BOING

ALEXANDER McCALL SMITH & ZOE PERSICO

There was something very strange about Jane.

When she was very small, she crawled – just like any other baby.

But when she grew a little bigger, she ... bounced!

Everybody was astonished. One moment Jane was on one side of the room – the next moment she was on the other.

"Did you see that?" asked her mother, in surprise.

"Yes," said her father. "I think she must have bounced!"

Over the next few days everybody watched Jane closely.

They saw her bounce out of bed and into the bathroom.

They saw her bounce downstairs and out into the garden.

Everywhere she went, she bounced – just like a rubber ball.

Her mother and father were a little bit worried. So they took her to the doctor, who looked closely at her feet and her toes. Then he took an X-ray photograph of the inside of her legs.

"My goodness!" exclaimed the doctor. "Look! This girl has springs in her knees!"

As she grew older, Jane found that she could bounce higher and higher.

She didn't mind if people looked at her.

If they stared too hard, she just bounced right over them.

That gave them something to think about!

At school it was useful being able to
bounce. She won all the high jump
competitions – very easily – and did
very well at other games too.

They called her Springy Jane now, as everybody knew she had springs in her knees.

There were many things Jane could do that other people could not.

Deep snow was no obstacle at all ...

And she could always get library books from the highest shelves – just by bouncing.

In fact, being able to bounce came in useful in all sorts of places.

Then one day there was the most terrible storm.

One old lady's house was completely surrounded by flood water, forcing her to take shelter on the roof. Nobody could reach her.

Then somebody said, "Send for Springy Jane!"

With a great effortless bounce, Jane landed exactly in the middle of the roof. She picked up the old lady in her arms and – One! Two! Three! – up she went, and down again, right over the water. What loud cheering there was!

Then, soaked to the skin, Jane bounced home and changed her clothes in front of the fire.

The next morning Jane felt a bit stiff. It was hard to bounce that day and she found she couldn't bounce very high at all.

Her parents took her back to the doctor, who tapped and prodded her knees and then shook his head.

"I'm sorry," he said. "Your springs got rusty in all that rain. I'll have to take them out. But don't worry, it won't hurt!"

With her springs removed, Jane couldn't bounce any more. But that didn't worry her. She found that it was good being able to walk just like anybody else. And the townsfolk just had to get used to using ladders again.

They still called her Springy Jane, though.

She liked this, because it was a nice name and it reminded her of how she used to bounce and how much fun it had been!

And as for the old lady ... She was so pleased at the exciting way Jane had rescued her that for her next birthday she made Jane a cake.

And there was something very odd about this cake – instead of candles, there were, yes, that's right ... icing sugar springs!

There was a large present too – a great big metal spring.

"Oh good!" said Jane. "I can bounce again."

And she did.

Grow a love of reading

PICTURE SQUIRRELS